JE Concept

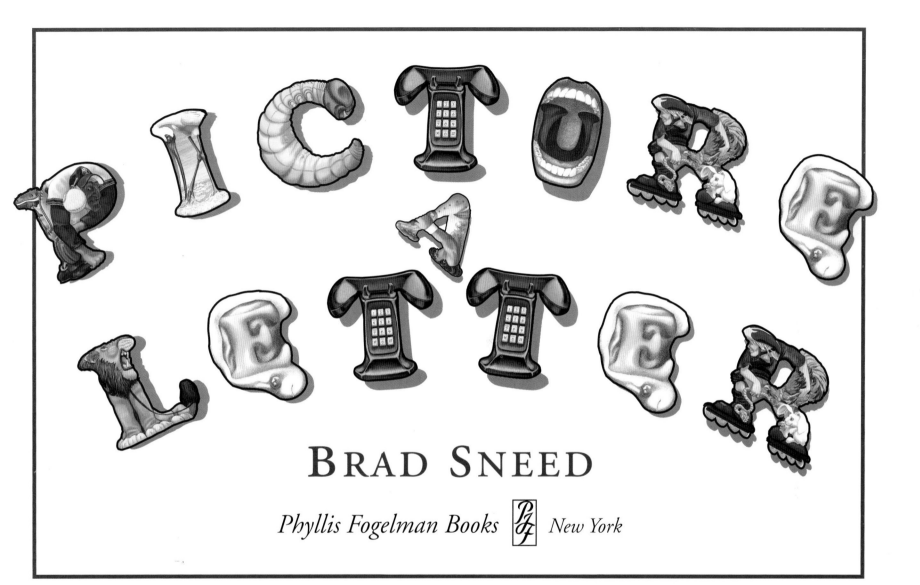

PICTURE A LETTER

BRAD SNEED

Phyllis Fogelman Books · *New York*

Published by Phyllis Fogelman Books
An imprint of Penguin Putnam Inc.
345 Hudson Street
New York, New York 10014

Copyright © 2002 by Bradley D. Sneed
All rights reserved
Designed by Nancy R. Leo-Kelly
Text set in Adobe Garamond
Printed in Hong Kong on acid-free paper
1 3 5 7 9 10 8 6 4 2

Library of Congress Cataloging-in-Publication Data
Sneed, Brad.
Picture a letter / Brad Sneed.
p.   cm.
ISBN 0-8037-2613-9
1. English language—Alphabet—Juvenile literature. [1. Alphabet.] I. Title.
PE1155 .S578 2002   [E]—dc21   2001023581

The artwork for this book was created with watercolor, gouache, colored pencil, and graphite on watercolor paper.

To all my young friends
who are learning the letters of the alphabet

A

A B

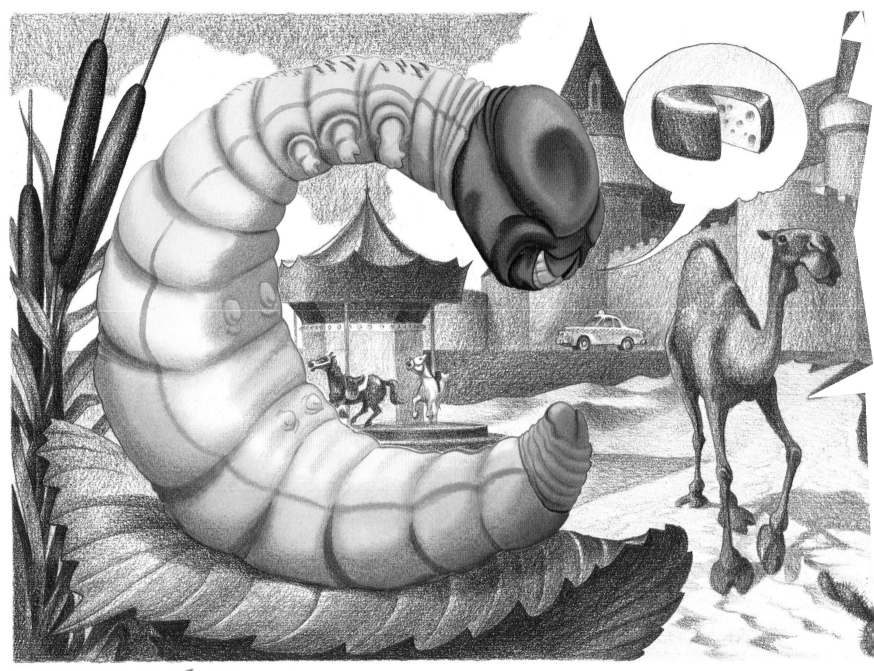

 A B C

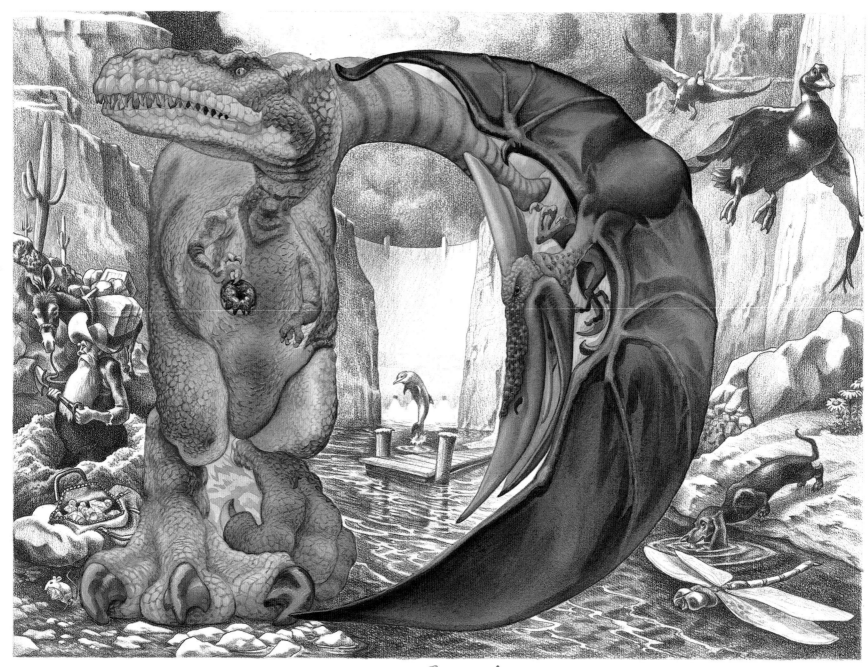

A B C D

A B C D E

A B C D E F

A B C D E F G

A B C D E F G H

A B C D E F G H

A B C D E F G H I

A B C D E F G H I J

A B C D E F G H I J K

A B C D E F G H I J K L M

A B C D E F G H I J K L M N

A B C D E F G H I J K L M N O

A B C D E F G H I J K L M N O P

A B C D E F G H I J K L M N O P

A B C D E F G H I J K L M N O P Q R

A B C D E F G H I J K L M N O P Q R

A B C D E F G H I J K L M N O P Q R S T

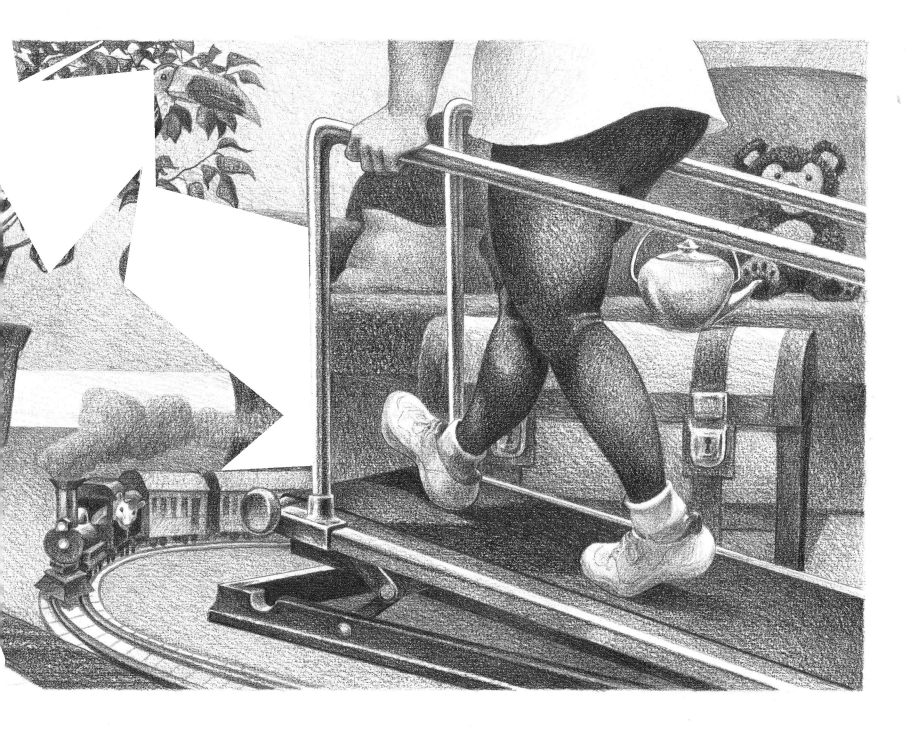

A B C D E F G H I J K L M N O P Q R S T

A B C D E F G H I J K L M N O P Q R S T U

A B C D E F G H I J K L M N O P Q R S T U V W

A B C D E F G H I J K L M N O P Q R S T U V W X **Y**

ABCDEFGHIJKLMNOPQRSTUVWXYZ

Accordion, **ACROBAT,** airplanes, aliens, alligator, angelfish, antennae, ape, apple, aquarium, archer, argyle socks, arrow, astronaut ❀ Bandage, **BANDANNA,** bandit, bank, bars, bat, batteries, beach, bee, belt, bird, blimp, boat, bolt, boots, bow, bowler, box, bricks, bridge, butterfly ❀ **Cab,** cactus, calf, camel, camera, cap, carousel, cartwheel, castle, **CATERPILLAR,** cattails, cheese, climb, cloud, corn, cow, crow ❀ Dachshund, daisies, dam, desert, diamonds, dig, **DINOSAURS,** dock, dolphin, donkey, doughnut, dragonfly, drink, ducks, duffel ❀ Eagle, **EAR,** earrings, earth, easel, eggs, elephant, elf, escalator, ewe, eye, eyebrow, eyelashes ❀ Falls, faucet, fawn, feather, fern, Ferris wheel, fillet knife, fire, fish, fishhooks, **FISHERMAN,** flashlight, flowers, fly, forest, fox, frog ❀ Gardener, gargoyles, gate, gazebo, ghost, glove, goat, **GOLF,** gondola, goose, gorilla, goslings, graduate, grass, grasshopper, graveyard ❀ Hair, hare, hat, hawk, haystacks, headphones, helicopter, heron, **HIPPOS,**

hoe, horse, horseshoe, hose, house, hula, hurdle, hydrant ❀ **IBIS,** icebergs, igloo, iguana, infant, inflate, initials, ink, inner tube, insect, inspect, island ❀ Jack-o'-lanterns, jaguar, jazz, jellyfish, **JESTER,** jewels, jingle bells, joust, jug, juggle, jungle ❀ Ka-choo, kangaroo, **KARATE,** kerchief, kettle, key, kick,

king, kitchen, kite, kitten, knob, knot, koala ❀ Lamp, lance, lariat, lattice, laugh, leapfrog, leash, lemon, lettuce, Lincoln, linguine, **LION,** loaf, lobster, locket, locomotive, loincloth, loop ❀ Macaw, magic wand, magician, mailman, marble, marionettes, marshmallows, matador, matches, monarch, **MONKEYS,** monocle, mustache ❀ Nail, nap, needle, needlepoint, nest, newspaper, night, nightlight, nose, **NURSE,** nursery, nursery rhyme, nutcracker, nuts ❀ Olive, onion, orange, **ORBIT,** Orion ❀ Pail, paint, paintbrush, painter, pandas, parachute, parrot, patch, peacock, peg leg, Pegasus,

pencil, pennants, picket fence, pirate, **PITCH,** plane, platypus, policeman, prairie dog, putt ❀ Quart, quarter, quarterback, **QUARTET,** queen, quill, quilt, quiver ❀ Rabbit, raccoon, race, raft, rapids, rat, razorback, rhinoceros, river, rocket, **ROLLERBLADE**® in-line skates, roller coaster, rooster, rope, rug, run ❀ Sailboat, sailor, sandal, sandwich, scuba diver, seagull, shark, sign, smile, snake, sneaker, snorkel, sock, squirrel, sunglasses, **SURF,** surfboard, swimmer ❀ Table, tablet, tadpole, talk, teapot, teddy bear, teeth, **TELEPHONE,** television, tennis, thimble, thread, toothbrush, toucan, train, treadmill, tree, trophy, trunk, tumbler ❀ U.F.O., umbrella, Uncle Sam, underwear, unicorn, unicycle, upside down, **UVULA** ❀ Vaccinate, vacuum, vampire, vase, veterinarian, vibrate, Viking, vine, violet, viper, vise, volcanoes, **VULTURE** ❀ Walrus, washboard, washtub, water, waves, web, well, whale, wheat, witch, **WORKHORSES** ❀ X ray, **XYLOPHONE** ❀ Yak, **YELL,** yolk, yo-yo ❀ Zebra, zeppelin, **ZEUS,** zipper